Naughty Scamper
Meets the Bush Monster

by
Penny Wooding

BREAKWATER

Breakwater
100 Water Street
P.O. Box 2188
St. John's, Newfoundland, Canada
A1C 6E6

This Newfoundland authored and illustrated book is published without any financial assistance whatsoever from the Publisher's Assistance Program administered by the Department of Culture, Recreation and Youth, Government of Newfoundland and Labrador.

The Publisher gratefully acknowledges the financial support of The Canada Council, which has helped make this publication possible.

Canadian Cataloguing in Publication Data

Wooding, Penny.

    Naughty Scamper meets the bush monster

    ISBN 1-55081-015-4

I. Title.

PS8595.052N33 1991   jC813'.54   C91-097544-2
PZ10.3.W66Na 1991

This book is dedicated to Silvia, Siân and Kelly; three eight-year-olds whose fascination with Naughty Scamper led to the writing of this story.

It was a glorious day at the barn! The sun shone and the animals smiled when Scamper gave his morning greeting.

"Good morning everyone! What a wonderful day! It's much too nice to stay in the barn. I'm going for a walk. Do you want to come?"

The animals were all so lazy under the heat of the summer sun.

"Oh no, Scamper," they said, "not today. Why waste energy when you can just laze around?"

"O.K! Suit yourselves," said Scamper, "but I'm not going to waste this lovely day away. See you later!"

With a kick of his heels, Scamper set off down the lane to the meadow. How good the flowers smelled. How fresh the air was. Scamper was a very happy horse on such a wonderful day.

Down the lane, Scamper saw his friend Jenny. She was out on her skateboard. She was having fun in the sun too.

"Hello Scamper," she called. "Look at my new skateboard. It goes so fast, I feel like I am flying!"

Scamper didn't even look at Jenny and her skateboard. He had seen something else!

Something was lurking in the bushes! Green shiny ears were sticking up through the leaves. Oh no! A bush monster!

Scamper could hardly believe his eyes. He gasped, he jumped, and he took off back towards the barn as fast as his legs could carry him!

"Look out!" shrieked Jenny, but it was too late. In his haste to escape from the terrible monster, Scamper sent Jenny— skateboard and all—flying into the ditch!

"You naughty Scamper!" cried Jenny, but Scamper
didn't hear a thing, he was already halfway back to the barn.

That night, Scamper told Nanny Cat all about his frightening experience. "It was just awful," he said, "I've never seen anything so ugly before!"

"Now Scamper," said Nanny Cat, "you really do make such a fuss! It was probably just a bird's nest or a mouse house!"

"No," said Scamper with an angry voice, "I tell you, I saw it! It was green and slimy; the yukkiest thing EVER!"

The next morning it was very windy. Scamper loved the wind. He was so happy, he forgot all about the ghastly bush monster.

"What a great day for a jog!" he said. "Does anyone want to come with me?"

"Oh no, Scamper," said the other animals. "Not today. We'd rather fly our kites in the wind."

So Scamper set off on his own again. How good the wind felt as it blew through his mane and tail!

"I wonder what it would be like to be a sailboat?" he thought.

"Hello Scamper," called Tommy as he rode by on his bicycle. "What are you doing out here on such a windy day?"

Scamper was miles away in his sailboat dream and didn't even see Tommy or his bicycle. He didn't see anything until suddenly...there it was again! An evil eye glaring from the monster bush!

"Oh no!" shrieked Scamper. "The bush monster! HELP!"

"Look out!" cried Tommy, but it was too late! Scamper spun around on his heels, sending Tommy and his bicycle flying into the ditch!

"You naughty Scamper!" screamed Tommy, but Scamper was already out of sight.

That night, Scamper told Nanny Cat the whole story.

"Really now, you are a silly Scamper sometimes," she meowed.

"Why?" asked Scamper.

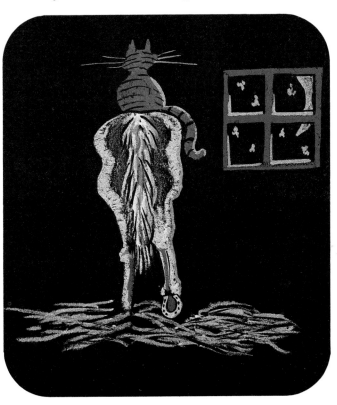

"Well," said Nanny Cat, "don't you think it is strange that the monster was in the exact same bush?"

"Not at all," said Scamper. "You have your favourite place on my back don't you? That bush must be his favourite bush!"

The next day it was raining. Scamper didn't like the rain.

"Maybe I won't go for a walk today," he said.

"Why don't you just go and see if your monster has gone?" said Nanny Cat.

"Maybe I should take a closer look," replied Scamper. "Will anyone come with me?"

"Not today," said the animals. "This is a good day for fishing!"

On his way down the lane, Scamper met Phyllis Farmer on her tractor. "Hello Scamper," she called. "What are you doing out on such a wet day with no raincoat on?"

Scamper didn't answer. He was getting close to the monster bush! As he slowly stepped forward, he could feel his knees and body shaking. Poor Scamper; he was so nervous!

Suddenly Scamper gasped! The green shiny ears were still there! Two evil eyes were glaring right at him through the bush! It was more than Scamper could stand! His shaky legs spun around and he started galloping back to the barn.

"Look out!" cried Phyllis, but it was too late; the tractor slipped on the wet mud and nose-dived into the ditch!

"You Naughty Scamper!" she screamed as she flew through the air.

"It's just no good!" said Scamper to Nanny Cat. "I'm just too afraid to face that monster on my own."

"But Scamper," said Nanny Cat, "you can't go through life being afraid of every little bush monster that comes your way. You have to face up to your fears!"

"Maybe if you came with me it would be easier. You could hiss at him and flash your sharp claws! Please come with me next time, Nanny Cat. Please!"

The next morning, Scamper woke up very early. He was so anxious about visiting the bush monster, he didn't even notice what the weather was like.

Doggy Dozo was still asleep as Scamper and Nanny Cat crept quietly out of the barn.

Scamper felt much braver now that he had his good friend with him.

"Thank you Nanny Cat" he said. "Thank you for coming with me."

"You're welcome." said Nanny Cat with a sigh. "Now Scamper, you watch the road carefully. I don't want to end up in the ditch today! Look out for Mr. Boggins and his bus!"

"Hello Mr. Boggins!" called Scamper.

"Hello Scamper! Hello Nanny Cat!" called Mr. Boggins. Scamper trotted merrily along with Nanny Cat on his back until they reached the monster's bush. Was he still there? Scamper slowed down and peered over the bush.

Yes! The monster was there!

"Oh no!" shrieked Scamper. His poor legs trembled and shook with fear. Nanny Cat was almost shaken right into the bush.

"I just can't stand it," screamed the terrified Scamper. "Hold tight Nanny Cat!"

Scamper was off in a flash and poor Nanny Cat got the biggest fright of all!

"Look out for the bus!" she cried, but it was too late. Mr. Boggins was already upside-down in the ditch!

"You naughty Scamper!" he yelled.

"Stop, Scamper, stop!" cried Nanny Cat. "Didn't you see what your monster really is?" Scamper screeched to a halt. "What do you mean?" he asked. "You saw it, didn't you? Isn't it green and slimy and ugly?"

"Really Scamper, you are silly some-times!" said Nanny Cat. "I saw something all right, but it wasn't a monster. Go back again and take a good look."

So, back to the bush they went again and Scamper did feel silly when he took a proper look. His monster was just a plain old green garbage bag!

"It must have fallen off the garbage truck into the bush!" said Nanny Cat.

Scamper just stared at the bag in amazement; then he smiled, and then he started to laugh! He laughed and he laughed and he laughed!

His laugh was so loud, all his friends from the town came rushing to see what had happened. When they saw the garbage bag monster they started to laugh too!

Jenny and Tommy laughed. Phyllis Farmer laughed. Mr. Boggins laughed, Nanny Cat and Doggy Dozo laughed.

"Well!" said Scamper when he recovered from his laughing attack, "Nanny Cat was right after all. I am a silly Scamper sometimes!"

Then, everyone laughed some more!